Cats
Are
Cats

poems compiled by Nancy Larrick

Philomel Books

MAR 8 9

drawings by Ed Young

New York

NORTHPORT PUBLIC LIBRARY
NORTHPORT, NEW YORK

Published in 1988 by Philomel Books,
a division of The Putnam & Grosset Group,
200 Madison Avenue, New York, NY 10016.
Original text copyright © 1988 by Nancy Larrick.
Illustrations copyright © 1988 by Ed Young.
All rights reserved.
Printed in Hong Kong by South China Printing Co.
Published simultaneously in Canada.
First impression

Library of Congress Cataloging-in-Publication Data
Cats are cats compiled by Nancy Larrick: illustrated by Ed Young.   p.   cm.
Summary: A collection of forty-two poems about all kinds of
cats, from old grumbling cats to proud cats who sit tall, by poets
including Eve Merriam, Jane Yolen, John Ciardi, and T.S. Eliot.
1. Cats—Juvenile poetry. 2. Children's poetry, American.
[1. Cats—Poetry. 2. American poetry—Collections.]
I. Larrick, Nancy. II. Young, Ed, ill.   PS595.C3813
1988   811'.5'0936—dc19   87-16728   CIP AC
ISBN 0-399-21517-4

In memory of Alec Crosby
and Rover,
the Cat who charmed our lives.
N.L.

For Mimi.
E.Y.

Contents

If You've Lived With a Cat...

If you've lived with a cat, you have come under the spell.

A silent presence moves in to survey the scene. Then to jump on the new velvet cushion, or curl up in grandmother's punch bowl.

Perhaps you've been awakened by your cat jolting the alarm clock to the floor and thumping defiantly down the hall. Asking to get out. Asking to get in.

Dancing in circles to catch its tail. Or into a kicking spin around your ball of yarn.

Hopping into the bed you are trying to make up—under the top sheet, then under the blanket, peering out to dare you to try again.

Gradually you learn that your cat makes the decisions, but so deftly, so graciously, so wisely that you give in. For despite the demands on your time and patience, you melt before that purring appreciation and understanding bestowed by cats on those who serve them.

Cats Are Cats is a collection of forty-two poems about such cats—dainty cats who tiptoe through the snow, old grumbling cats, snarling cats who fight in a dark alley, demanding cats who take center stage, curious cats who poke and prowl, proud cats who sit tall.

These are cats who have won the loyalty and love of the poets. I hope they win your heart too.

Nancy Larrick

My Cat, Mrs. Lick-a-Chin

Some of the cats I know about
Spend a little time in and a lot of time out.
Or a lot of time out and a little time in.
But *my* cat, Mrs. Lick-a-chin,
Never knows *where* she wants to be.
If I let her in she looks at me
And begins to sing that she wants to go out.
So I open the door and she looks about
And begins to sing, "Please let me in!"

Poor silly Mrs. Lick-a-chin!

The thing about cats, as you may find,
Is that no one knows what they have in mind.

And I'll tell you something about that:
No one knows it less than my cat.

John Ciardi

The Open Door

Out of the dark
to the sill of the door
lay the snow in a long
unruffled floor,
and the lamplight fell
narrow and thin
a carpet unrolled
for the cat to walk in.
Slowly, smoothly,
black as the night,
with paws unseen
(white upon white)
like a queen who walks
down a corridor
the black cat paced
that cold smooth floor—
and left behind her,
bead upon bead,
the track of small feet
little dark fern seed.

Elizabeth Coatsworth

Cat in Moonlight

Through moonlight's milk
She slowly passes
As soft as silk
Between tall grasses.
I watch her go
So sleek and white,
As white as snow,
The moon so bright
I hardly know
White moon, white fur,
Which is the light
And which is her.

Douglas Gibson

Cat at Night

The cat in moonlight
takes his shadow with him
over the fence
and loses it under the cottonwoods.

Adrien Stoutenburg

On a Night of Snow

Cat, if you go outdoors you must walk in the snow,
You will come back with little white shoes on your feet,
Little white slippers of snow that have heels of sleet.
Stay by the fire, my Cat. Lie still, do not go.
See how the flames are leaping and hissing low,
I will bring you a saucer of milk like a marguerite,
So white and so smooth, so spherical and so sweet—
Stay with me, Cat. Out-doors the wild winds blow.

Out-doors the wild winds blow, Mistress, and dark is the night.
Strange voices cry in the trees, intoning strange lore
And more than cats move, lit by our eyes' green light,
On silent feet where the meadow grasses hang hoar—
Mistress, there are portents abroad of magic and might,
And things that are yet to be done. Open the door!

Elizabeth Coatsworth

16

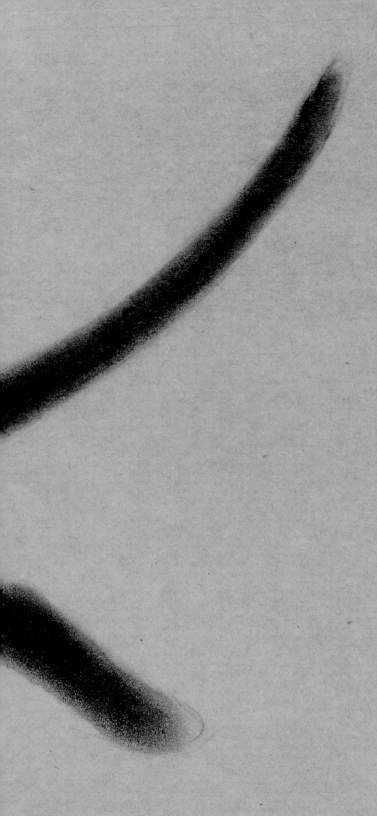

That Cat

That cat is crazy
Just a bit
Elegant
Mysterious
Dancing on the midnight grasses
Moonlit
Very royal
Delirious.

Karla Kuskin

17

18

Wanted—A Witch's Cat

Wanted—a witch's cat,
Must have vigor and spite,
Be expert at hissing,
And good in a fight,
And have balance and poise
On a broomstick at night.

Wanted—a witch's cat,
Must have hypnotic eyes
To tantalize victims
And mesmerize spies,
And be adept
At scanning the skies.

Wanted—a witch's cat,
With a sly, cunning smile,
And knowledge of spells
And a good deal of guile,
With a fairly hot temper
And plenty of bile.

Wanted—a witch's cat,
Who's not afraid to fly,
For a cat with strong nerves
The salary's high
Wanted—a witch's cat;
Only the best need apply.

Shelagh McGee

The Stray Cat

It's just an old alley cat
that has followed us all the way home.

It hasn't a star on its forehead,
or a silky satiny coat.

No proud tiger stripes, no dainty tread,
no elegant velvet throat.

It's a splotchy, blotchy
city cat, not a pretty cat,
a rough little tough little bag of old bones.

"Beauty," we shall call you.
"Beauty, come in."

Eve Merriam

The Lost Cat

She took a last and simple meal when there were none to
    see her steal—
  A jug of cream upon the shelf, a fish prepared for
    dinner;
And now she walks a distant street with delicately
    sandalled feet,
  And no one gives her much to eat or weeps to see her
    thinner.

O my belovèd come again, come back in joy, come back
    in pain,
  To end our searching with a mew, or with a purr our
    grieving;
And you shall have for lunch or tea whatever fish swim
    in the sea
  And all the cream that's meant for me—and not a
    word of thieving!

E. V. Rieu

Tom Cat

This cat, see, yellow
like an old man's eye,
slunk behind a garbage can
slam-rattle, slam-bang!
He pushed that lid off,
leapt inside,
tail whipped back and forth
and a sound like a kid's toy motor
started—stopped, started—stopped.

This kid came zap-dapping
down the street,
hat jammed on eyes,
shoulders hustling along,
he clamped that lid down tight,
kicked the can
and walked on out.

I waited 'til that busted
hat was gone
and tore that lid off—
I'm telling you
it was like lifting the top
of a spaghetti pot
with the steam puffing out.
That cat kept roaring and purring,
the sound smoking up in the cold air.

I could've warmed my whole body.

Ann Turner

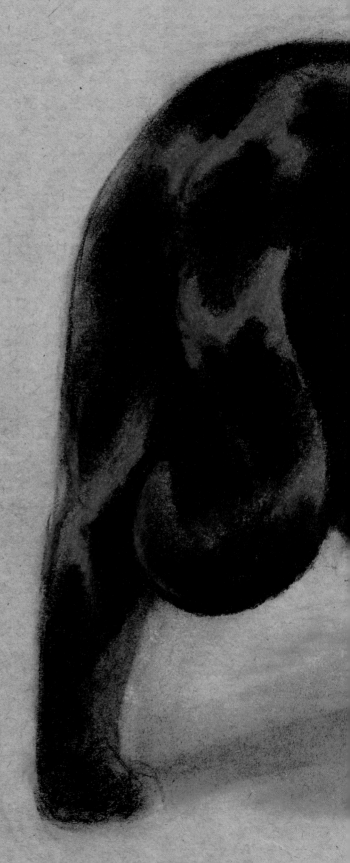

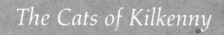

The Cats of Kilkenny

There were once two cats of Kilkenny,
Each thought there was one cat too many;
So they fought and they fit,
And they scratched and they bit,
Till, excepting their nails
And the tips of their tails,
Instead of two cats, there weren't any.

Anonymous

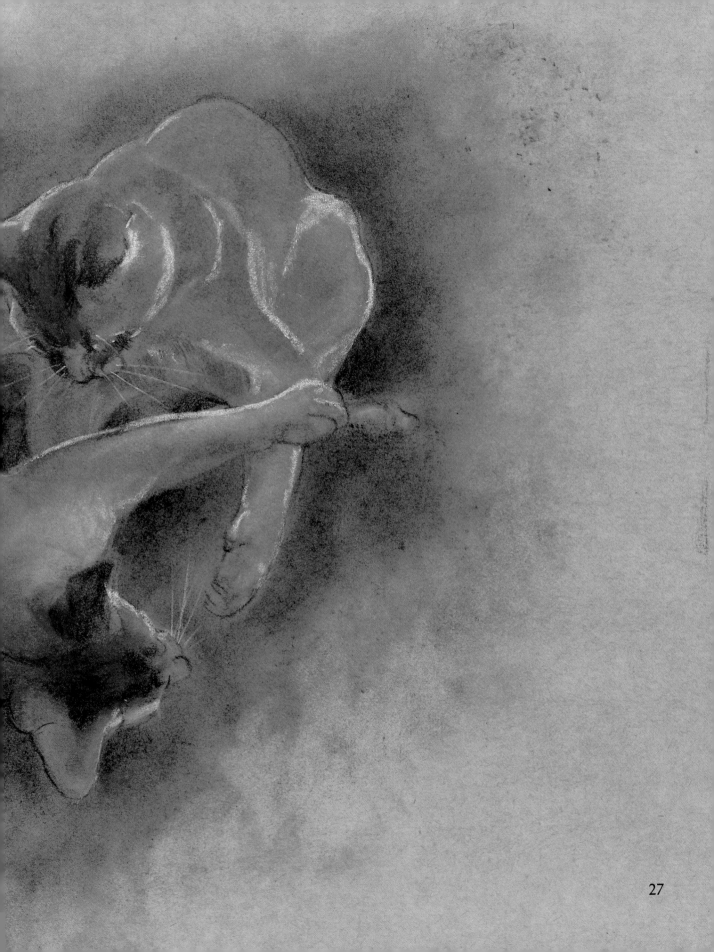

The Tomcat

At midnight in the alley
A Tomcat comes to wail,
And he chants the hate of a million years
As he swings his snaky tail.

Malevolent, bony, brindled,
Tiger and devil and bard,
His eyes are coals from the middle of Hell
And his heart is black and hard.

He twists and crouches and capers
And bares his curved sharp claws,
And he sings to the stars of the jungle nights,
Ere cities were, or laws.

Beast from a world primeval,
He and his leaping clan,
When the blotched red moon leers over the roofs,
Give voice to their scorn of man.

He will lie on a rug tomorrow
And lick his silky fur,
And veil the brute in his yellow eyes
And play he's tame, and purr.

But at midnight in the alley
He will crouch again and wail,
And beat the time for his demon's song
with the swing of his demon's tail.

Don Marquis

28

Rescue

Bony cat,
Scrabbling along
In the sleet,
You need a child
To warm you.
I'll take you, cat,
Where it's dry,
And there's a can of milk.
I'll feed you, Bony.
We'll be friends.
No more hiding
Under cars,
No more crying.
We'll be friends,
Bony cat,
Scrabbling along
In the sleet.

Virginia Schonborg

Alley Cat School

Do alley cats go
   to alley cat school?
Where they learn how to slink
   and stay out all night?
Where they learn how to find
   warm and comfortable places?
On a cold wintry night?
Do they learn from teachers and books
   how to topple a garbage can lid?
Did they all go
   to alley cat school?
Is that what they did?

Frank Asch

One O'clock

One of the Clock, and silence deep
Then up the Stairway, black and steep
The old House-Cat comes creepy-creep
With soft feet goes from room to room
Her green eyes shining through the gloom,
  And finds all fast asleep.

Katharine Pyle

This Cat

This cat
Walks into the room and across the floor,
Under a chair, around the bed,
Behind the table and out the door.
I'm sitting on the chair
And I don't see where he is.
I don't see one hair of his.
I just hear the floorboards scarcely squeak.
This cat comes and goes
On invisible toes.
The sneak.

Karla Kuskin

33

Our Cat

The cat goes out
   And the cat comes back
And no one can follow
   Upon her track.
She knows where she's going,
   She knows where she's been,
And all we can do
   Is to let her in.

Marchette Chute

Cat

Old Mog comes in and sits on the newspaper
Old fat sociable cat
Thinks when we stroke him he's doing us a favour
Maybe he's right, at that.

                                        Joan Aiken

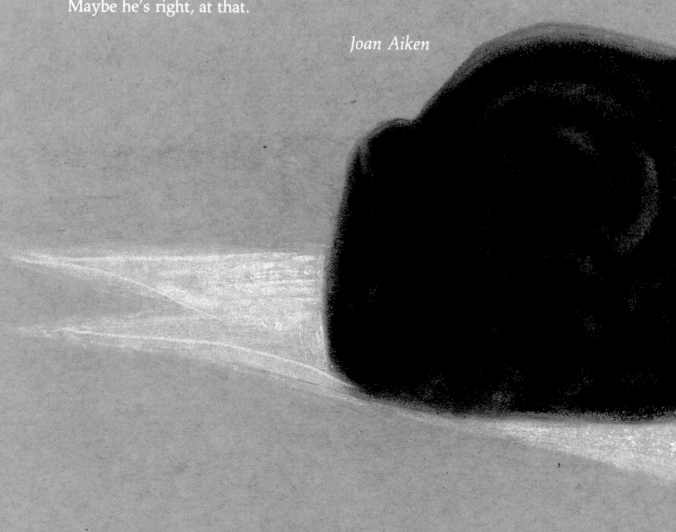

Pictures of Cats

Examining the breeze.
A package neatly wrapped with tail
Flicks a whisker
Pleased.

Upon the stair.
Taking the air.
Unquestioned owner
Of the comfortable chair.

Napping everywhere
Stretched in the sun
As if the sun were hers
Awash in warmth
And furs.

The flow of a cat walking
Over the lawn
To place herself like a soft stone
In the middle of the paper
I am working on.

Karla Kuskin

Chang McTang McQuarter Cat

Chang McTang McQuarter Cat
Is one part this and one part that.
One part is yowl, one part is purr.
One part is scratch, one part is fur.
One part, maybe even two,
Is how he sits and stares right through
You and you and you and you.
And when you feel my Chang-Cat stare
You wonder if you're really there.

Chang McTang McQuarter Cat
Is one part this and ten parts that.
He's one part saint, and two parts sin.
One part yawn, and three parts grin,
One part sleepy, four parts lightning,
One part cuddly, five parts fright'ning,
One part snarl, and six parts play.
One part is how he goes away
Inside himself, somewhere miles back
Behind his eyes, somewhere as black
And green and yellow as the night
A jungle makes in full moonlight.

40

Chang McTang McQuarter Cat
Is one part this and twenty that.
One part is statue, one part tricks—
(One part, or six, or thirty-six.)

One part (or twelve, or sixty-three)
Is—Chang McTang belongs to ME!
Don't ask, "how many parts is that?"
Addition's nothing to a cat.

If you knew Chang, then you'd know this:
He's one part everything there is.

John Ciardi

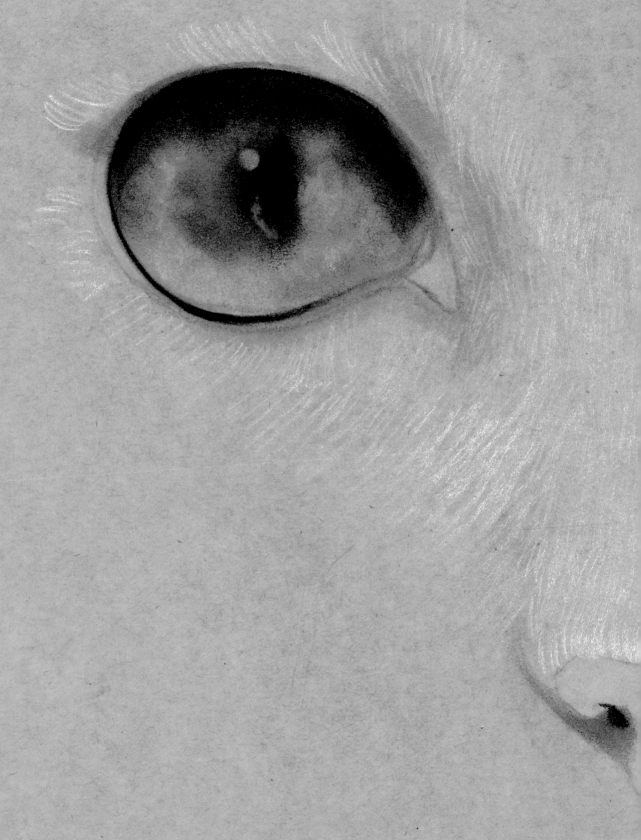

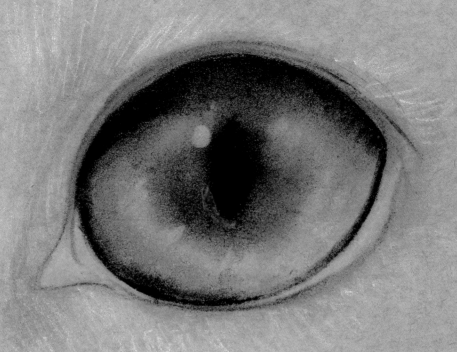

True

When
the green eyes
of a cat
look deep into
you

you know
that
whatever it is
they are saying
is
true.

Lilian Moore

The Mysterious Cat

I saw a proud, mysterious cat,
I saw a proud, mysterious cat,
Too proud to catch a mouse or rat—
Mew, mew, mew.

But catnip she would eat, and purr,
But catnip she would eat, and purr,
And goldfish she did much prefer—
Mew, mew, mew.

I saw a cat—'twas but a dream,
I saw a cat—'twas but a dream,
Who scorned the slave that brought her cream—
Mew, mew, mew.

Unless the slave were dressed in style,
Unless the slave were dressed in style,
And knelt before her all the while—
Mew, mew, mew.

Did you ever hear of a thing like that?
Did you ever hear of a thing like that?
Did you ever hear of a thing like that?
Oh, what a proud, mysterious cat.
Oh, what a proud, mysterious cat.
Oh, what a proud, mysterious cat.
Mew . . . mew . . . mew.

Vachel Lindsay

45

What the Gray Cat Sings

The Cat was once a weaver,
   A weaver, a weaver,
An old and withered weaver
  Who labored late and long;
And while she made the shuttle hum
And wove the weft and clipped the thrum,
Beside the loom with droning drum
   She sang the weaving song:
     "Pr-rrum, pr-rrum,
Thr-ree thr-reads in the thr-rum,
    Pr-rrum!"

The Cat's no more a weaver
  A weaver, a weaver,
An old and wrinkled weaver,
  For though she did no wrong,
A witch hath changed the shape of her
That dwindled down and clothed in fur
Beside the hearth with droning purr
   She thrums her weaving song:
     "Pr-rrum, pr-rrum,
Thr-ree thr-reads in the thr-rum,
    Pr-rrum!"

Arthur Guiterman

If . . . .

If you,
Like me,
Were made of fur
And sun warmed you,
Like me,
You'd purr.

Karla Kuskin

47

Rosalie the Cat

Julia loves her Rosalie.
Rosalie the cat.
Julia pets her nosealie.
Soft, disdainful Rosalie.
Steps upon her toesalie
Pulls her tail and
Ohsalie
Julia has a scratch.

While Rosalie guileless
And practically smileless
Suns quietly, sly on her mat.

Karla Kuskin

Cat Cat

Cat cat cat on the bed,
Bed's too soft, it jumps on my head.
Head head, head's too hard,
Cat wriggles out into the yard.
Yard yard, cat slips away
Over to the playground where the children play.
Playground seesaw, who wants to ride?
Cat's all ready on the other side.

Eve Merriam

Cat!

     Cat!
     Scat!
Atter her, atter her,
Sleeky flatterer,
Spitfire chatterer,
Scatter her, scatter her,
     Off her mat!
     Wuff!
     Wuff!
     Treat her rough!
Git her, git her,
Whiskery spitter!
Catch her, catch her,
Green-eyed scratcher!

Slathery
Slithery
Hisser,
Don't miss her!
Run till you're dithery,
Hithery
Thithery!
Pfitts! pfitts!
How she spits!
Spitch! Spatch!
Can't she scratch!
Scritching the bark
Of the sycamore-tree,
She's reached her ark
And's hissing at me
  Pfitts! pfitts!
  Wuff! wuff!
    Scat,
    Cat!
    That's
    That!

Eleanor Farjeon

51

Lew and Lee

Two cats were sitting in a tree,
kritte vitte vit bom bom,
a cat called Lew,
a cat called Lee,
kritte vitte vit bom bom.
"Now follow me,"
said Lew to Lee,
kritte vitte vitte vitte vit bom bom,
for I no longer like this tree,
kritte vitte vit bom bom!

So Lew and Lee
climbed down the tree,
kritte vitte vit bom bom.
Once down the tree
to Lew said Lee,
kritte vitte vit bom bom,
"Oh, Lew, I rather like that tree!"
kritte vitte vitte vitte vit bom bom.
So Lew and Lee climbed up the tree,
Kritte vitte vit bom bom!

Danish nursery rhyme
translated by N. M. Bodecker

A Different Door

When rain stays, gray and unabating,
And long kept in he stares out, waiting,
And no one heeds and starts unlatching
Our back door, Tom tries front door-scratching.

That cat, he's not what you'd call bright—
Still, for a chance, however slight,
At wren-songed skies where rainbows soar,
Who wouldn't scratch some different door?

X. J. Kennedy

cat bath

In the midst
Of grooming
Her inner
Thigh,

Her leg
Locked
High at
Her back,

She looks
Up: with
A pink
Crescent

Tongue
Left
Between lip
And lip.

Valerie Worth

The Song of the Jellicles

Jellicle Cats come out tonight,
Jellicle Cats come one come all:
The Jellicle Moon is shining bright—
Jellicles come to the Jellicle Ball.

Jellicle Cats are black and white,
Jellicle Cats are rather small;
Jellicle Cats are merry and bright,
And pleasant to hear when they caterwaul.
Jellicle Cats have cheerful faces,
Jellicle Cats have bright black eyes;
They like to practise their airs and graces
And wait for the Jellicle Moon to rise.

Jellicle Cats develop slowly,
Jellicle Cats are not too big;
Jellicle Cats are roly-poly,
They know how to dance a gavotte and a jig.
Until the Jellicle Moon appears
They make their toilette and take their repose:
Jellicles wash behind their ears,
Jellicles dry between their toes.

Jellicle Cats are white and black,
Jellicle Cats are of moderate size;
Jellicles jump like a jumping-jack,
Jellicle Cats have moonlit eyes.
They're quiet enough in the morning hours,
They're quiet enough in the afternoon.
Reserving their terpsichorean powers
To dance by the light of the Jellicle Moon.

Jellicle Cats are black and white,
Jellicle Cats (as I said) are small;
If it happens to be a stormy night
They will practise a caper or two in the hall.
If it happens the sun is shining bright
You would say they have nothing to do at all:
They are resting and saving themselves to be right
For the Jellicle Moon and the Jellicle Ball.

T. S. Eliot

The Cat Heard the Cat-Bird

One day, a fine day, a high-flying-sky day,
A cat-bird, a fat bird, a fine fat cat-bird
Was sitting and singing on a stump by the
    highway.
Just sitting. And singing. Just that. But a
    cat heard.

A thin cat, a grin-cat, a long thin grin-cat
Came creeping the sly way by the highway to
    the stump.
"Oh cat-bird, the cat heard! O cat-bird scat!
The grin-cat is creeping! He's going to jump!"

—One day, a fine day, a high-flying-sky day
A fat cat, yes, that cat we met as a thin cat
Was napping, cat-napping, on a stump by the
    highway,
And even in his sleep you could see he was a
    grin-cat.

Why was he grinning? —He must have had a
    dream.
What made him so fat? —A pan full of cream.
What about the cat-bird? —What bird, dear?
I don't see any cat-bird here.

John Ciardi

Apartment Cats

The Girls wake, stretch, and pad up to the door.
    They rub my leg and purr;
    One sniffs around my shoe,
    Rich with an outside smell,
  The other rolls back on the floor—
White bib exposed, and stomach of soft fur.

Now, more awake, they re-enact Ben Hur
    Along the corridor,
    Wheel, gallop; as they do,
    Their noses twitching still,
  Their eyes get wild, their bodies tense,
Their usual prudence seemingly withdraws.

And then they wrestle: parry, lock of paws,
    Blind hug of close defense,
    Tail-thump, and smothered mew.
    If either, though, feels claws,
  She abruptly rises, knowing well
How to stalk off in wise indifference.

Thom Gunn

Montague Michael

Montague Michael
You're much too fat,
You wicked old, wily old,
Well-fed cat.

All night you sleep
On a cushion of silk,
And twice a day
I bring you milk.

And once in a while,
When you catch a mouse,
You're the proudest person
In all the house.

Anonymous

Cats Sleep Fat

Cats sleep fat and walk thin.
Cats, when they sleep, slump;
When they wake, stretch and begin
Over, pulling their ribs in.
Cats walk thin.

Cats wait in a lump,
Jump in a streak.
Cats, when they jump, are sleek
As a grape slipping its skin—
They have technique.
Oh, cats don't creak.
They sneak.

Cats sleep fat.
They spread out comfort underneath them
Like a good mat,
As if they picked the place
And then sat;
You walk around one
As if he were the City Hall
After that.

Rosalie Moore
(from "Catalogue")

The King of Cats
Sends a Postcard to His Wife

Keep your whiskers crisp and clean.
Do not let the mice grow lean.
Do not let yourself grow fat
like a common kitchen cat.

Have you set the kittens free?
Do they sometimes ask for me?
Is our catnip growing tall?
Did you patch the garden wall?

Clouds are gentle walls that hide
gardens on the other side.
Tell the tabby cats I take
all my meals with William Blake,

lunch at noon and tea at four,
served in splendor on the shore
at the tinkling of a bell.
Tell them I am sleeping well.

Tell them I have come so far,
brought by Blake's celestial car,
buffeted by wind and rain,
I may not get home again.

Take this message to my friends.
Say the King of Catnip sends
to the cat who winds his clocks
a thousand sunsets in a box,

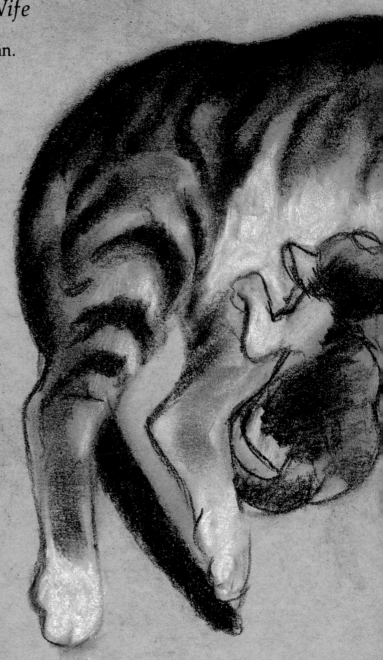

to the cat who brings the ice
the shadows of a dozen mice
(serve them with assorted dips
and eat them like potato chips),

and to the cat who guards his door
a net for catching stars, and more
(if with patience he abide):
catnip from the other side.

Nancy Willard

Sing a Song of Kittens

Sing a song of kittens,
Kittens full of play,
Chasing shadows, chasing tails,
Romping half the day,
Springing upon—nothing!
Scampering off—nowhere!
Glaring out of milk-blue eyes,
Lashing tails in air.

Sing a song of kittens,
Kittens tired of play,
Kittens growing sleepy
At the close of day.
Very glad to cuddle,
Very pleased to purr,
Curling up in little balls
Of thistledown and fur.

Elizabeth Coatsworth

Mother Cat's Purr

Sleep the half-sleep,
Kittens dear,
While your mother
Cat-naps near.

Every kitten
Is a cat,
And you must
Remember that

Naps for cats
Are mostly fake:
Any time
Is time to wake,

Or time to pounce,
Or time to scat.
That's what sleep is—
For a cat.

Jane Yolen

Confidence

Little cats walk with their tails up.
Happy, they are afraid of nothing.
They will hiss at a big dog or a big person,
Not to defend themselves,
But to show their spirit.

Martha Baird

kitten

The black kitten,
Arched stiff,
Dances sidewise
From behind
The chair, leaps,
Tears away with
Ears back, spins,
Lands crouched
Flat on the floor,
Sighting something
At nose level,
Her eyes round
As oranges, her
Hind legs marking
Time: then she
Pounces, cactus-
Clawed, upon
A strayed
Strand of fluff:
Can anyone
Believe that she
Doesn't ask us
To laugh?

Valerie Worth

A Kitten

"A kitten, a black one,
is all I want," I said.
Mother looked at Father
and sort of shook her head.
"Of course, I'd take a pony.
I'd take a cow or pig,
billy goat, a nanny goat,
and several not so big.
I'd take a hen and rooster,
a turkey that could strut;
I'd even take a CROCODILE . . ."
But Mother said, "Tut, tut—
Goats may have their good points,
pigs, and roosters, too,
but don't you think a little cat,
a blackish one, would do?"

Aileen Fisher

73

Cat

Cats are not at all like people,
  Cats are Cats.

People wear stockings and sweaters,
Overcoats, mufflers, and hats.
Cats wear nothing: they lie by the fire
For twenty-four hours if they desire.
They do NOT rush out of the office,
They do NOT have interminable chats,
They do NOT play Old Maid and Checkers,
They do NOT wear bright yellow spats.

People, of course, will always be people,
  But Cats are Cats

William Jay Smith

Copyright Acknowledgments

Philomel Books would like to thank the following for permission to reprint the selections in this book. All possible care has been taken to trace the ownership of every selection included and to make full acknowledgment for its use. If any errors have accidentally occurred, they will be corrected in subsequent editions provided notification is sent to the publishers:

Associated Book Publishers (U.K.) Ltd., for "The Lost Cat" by E.V. Rieu from *The Flattered Flying Fish and Other Poems.* Copyright 1962 by E.V. Rieu. Reprinted by permission of E.V. Rieu, Associated Book Publishers Ltd. and Methuen & Co.

Atheneum Publishers, for "A Different Door" by X.J. Kennedy from *The Forgetful Wishing Well.* Copyright © 1985 by X.J. Kennedy (A Margaret K. McElderry Book.) Reprinted with the permission of Atheneum Publishers.

Atheneum Publishers, for "True" by Lilian Moore from *I Feel The Same Way.* Copyright © 1967 by Lilian Moore. Reprinted by permission of Atheneum Publishers, a division of Macmillan, Inc.

Atheneum Publishers, for "Two Cats Were Sitting in a Tree" by N.M. Bodecker from *It's Raining, Said John Twaining: Danish Rhymes.* Copyright © 1973 by N.M. Bodecker. (A Margaret K. McElderry Book.) Reprinted with the permission of Atheneum Publishers, an imprint of Macmillan Publishing Co.

Catherine Barnes, for "On a Night of Snow" by Elizabeth Coatsworth from *Night and The Cat.* Copyright © 1950 by Elizabeth Coatsworth. Reprinted by permission of Catherine Barnes.

Bell & Hyman, England, for "Cat in Moonlight" by Douglas Gibson from *Happy Landings.* Copyright © 1971 by Douglas Gibson. Reprinted with the permission of Bell & Hyman.

Curtis Brown, Ltd, for "Cat at Night" from *Things That Are* by Adrien Stoutenburg. Copyright © 1964 by Reilly & Lee. Reprinted by permission of Curtis Brown, Ltd.

Curtis Brown Ltd., for "Mother Cat's Purr" by Jane Yolen from *Dragon Night and Other Lullabies.* Copyright © 1981 by Jane Yolen. Reprinted by permission of Curtis Brown Ltd.

Marchette Chute, for "Our Cat" by Marchette Chute. Reprinted from *Rhymes About Us* by Marchette Chute. Copyright © 1974. By permission of the author.

Delacorte Press, for "Cat" by William Jay Smith from *Laughing Time.* Copyright © 1980 by William Jay Smith. Reprinted with the permission of Delacorte Press.

Dell Publishing, for "The Stray Cat" by Eve Merriam from *Jamboree.* Copyright © 1984 by Eve Merriam. Reprinted by permission of Dell Publishing.

Doubleday, for "The Tomcat" by Don Marquis from *Poems and Portraits.* Copyright © 1917 by Sun Printing & Publishing. Reprinted by permission of Doubleday Publishing, a division of Bantam, Doubleday, Dell Publishing Group.

Farrar, Straus, Giroux, for "Apartment Cats" by Thom Gunn from *Molly and My Sad Captain.* Copyright © 1961 by Thom Gunn. Reprinted with the permission of Farrar, Straus, Giroux.

Farrar, Straus, Giroux, for "Cat Bath" by Valerie Worth from *Still More Small Poems.* Copyright © 1978 by Valerie Worth. Reprinted with the permission of Farrar, Straus, Giroux.

Farrar, Straus, Giroux, for "Kitten" by Valerie Worth from *More Small Poems.* Copyright © 1976 by Valerie Worth. Reprinted with the permission of Farrar, Straus, Giroux.

Grosset & Dunlap, for "Sing a Song of Kittens" by Elizabeth Coatsworth from *The Sparrow Bush.* Copyright © 1966 by Grosset & Dunlap. Reprinted by permission of Grosset & Dunlap, Inc.

Harcourt Brace Jovanovich, Inc., for "The King of the Cats Sends a Postcard to His Wife" by Nancy Willard from *A Visit to William Blake's Inn.* Copyright © 1981 by Nancy Willard. Reprinted with permission from Harcourt Brace Jovanovich, Inc.

Harcourt Brace Jovanovich, Inc., and Faber and Faber, Ltd., for "The Song of the Jellicles" by T.S. Eliot from *Old Possom's Book of Practical Cats.* Copyright © 1939 by T.S. Eliot. Renewed 1967 by Esme Valerie Eliot. Reprinted by permission of Harcourt Brace Jovanovich, Inc., and Faber & Faber, Ltd.

Harper & Row, Publishers, Inc., for "One o'clock" from *The Wonder Clock* by Howard Pyle with verses by Katharine Pyle. Copyright © 1887 by Harper & Row, publishers, Inc. Copyright renewed, 1915, by Anne Poole Pyle. Reprinted by permission of Harper & Row, Publishers, Inc.

Harper & Row, publishers, Inc., for "My Cat, Mrs. Lick-a-chin" from *You Read To Me, I'll Read To You* by John Ciardi. Copyright © 1962 by John Ciardi. Reprinted by permission of Harper & Row, Publishers, Inc.

Harper & Row, Publishers, Inc., for "That cat is crazy" from *Near The Window Tree* by Karla Kuskin. Copyright © 1975 by Karla Kuskin. Reprinted by permission of Harper & Row, Publishers, Inc.

Harper & Row, Publishers, Inc., for "This Cat" from *Dogs, Dragons, Trees and Dreams* by Karla Kuskin. Originally appeared in *Near The Window Tree,* copyright © 1975 Karla Kuskin. Reprinted by permission of Harper & Row, Publishers, Inc.

Harper & Row, Publishers, Inc., for "Confidence" from *The Other Side of a Poem* by Barbara Abercrombie. Copyright © 1977 Barbara Mattes Abercrombie. Reprinted by permission of Harper & Row, Publishers, Inc.

Harper & Row, Publishers, Inc., for "A Kitten" from *Feathered Ones and Furry* by Aileen Fisher. Originally published in *That's Why* by Aileen Fisher. Copyright © 1946 by Aileen Fisher. Reprinted by permission of Harper & Row, Publishers, Inc.

Harper & Row, Publishers, Inc., for "Cat" from *Eleanor Farjeon's Poems For Children*. Originally published in *Sing For Your Supper* by Eleanor Farjeon. Copyright © 1938, renewed 1966. Reprinted by permission of Harper & Row, Publishers, Inc.

Harper & Row, Publishers, Inc., for "Chang McTang McQuarter Cat" from *You Read To Me, I'll Read To You* by John Ciardi. Copyright © 1962 by John Ciardi. Reprinted by permission of Harper & Row, Publishers, Inc.

Harper & Row, Publishers, Inc., for "If You" from *Dogs, Dragons, Trees and Dreams* by Karla Kuskin. Originally appeared in *Any Me I Want To Be* by Karla Kuskin. Copyright © 1972 Karla Kuskin. Reprinted by permission of Harper & Row, Publishers, Inc.

Harper & Row, Publishers, Inc., for "Julia Loves Her Rosalie" from *Near The Window Tree* by Karla Kuskin. Copyright © 1975 by Karla Kuskin. Reprinted by permission of Harper & Row, Publishers, Inc.

Harper & Row, Publishers, Inc., for "Examining the Breeze" fron *Near The Window Tree* by Karla Kuskin. Copyright © 1975 by Karla Kuskin. Reprinted by permission of Harper & Row, Publishers, Inc.

Hodder & Stoughton, Australia, for "Montague Michael" from FOR ME, ME, ME: *Poems For The Very Young*. Copyright © 1983 by Hodder & Stoughton. Reprinted with the permission of Hodder & Stoughton.

Houghton Mifflin Company, for "The Cat Heard the Cat-Bird" from *I Met a Man* by John Ciardi. Copyright © 1961 by John Ciardi. Reprinted by permission of Houghton Mifflin Company.

Houghton Mifflin Company, for "Tom Cat" from *Street Talk* by Ann Turner. Copyright © 1986 by Ann Turner. Reprinted by permission of Houghton Mifflin Company.

Macmillan Publishing Company, for "The Open Door" from *Away Goes Sally* by Elizabeth Coatsworth. Copyright © 1934 by Macmillan Publishing Company, renewed 1962 by Elizabeth Coatsworth Beston. Reprinted with permission of Macmillan Publishing Company.

Macmillan Publishing Company, for "The Mysterious Cat" from *Collected Poems* by Vachel Lindsay. Copyright © 1914 by Macmillan Publishing Company, renewed 1942 by Elizabeth C. Lindsay. Reprinted by permission of Macmillan Publishing Company.

Shelagh McGee, for "Wanted—A Witch's Cat" from *What Witches Do* by Shelagh McGee. Copyright © 1980 by Felix Gluck Press, Ltd. Reprinted by permission of the author.

William Morrow & Company, Inc. for "Rescue" for *Subway Singer*. Copyright © 1970 by Virginia Schonborg. Reprinted by permission of William Morrow & Company, Inc.

William Morrow & Company, Inc., for "Alley Cat School" from *City Sandwich*. Copyright © 1978 by Frank Asch. Reprinted by permission of Greenwillow Books, a division of William Morrow.

The New Yorker, for "Catalogue" by Rosalie Moore. Copyright © 1940, 1968 by The New Yorker. Reprinted by permission of The New Yorker.

Marian Reiner, for "Cat cat cat on the bed . . ." from *Blackberry Ink* by Eve Merriam. Copyright © 1985 by Eve Merriam. All rights reserved. Reprinted by permission of Marian Reiner for the author.

Louise H. Sclove, for "What the Grey Cat Sings" from *I Sing The Pioneer* by Arthur Guiterman. Copyright © 1926 by Arthur Guiterman. Reprinted by permission of Louise H. Sclove.

Viking Penguin, Inc., for "Cat" from *The Skin Spinners* by Joan Aiken. Copyright © 1960, 1973, 1974, 1975, 1976 by Joan Aiken. All rights reserved. Reprinted by permission of Viking Penguin, Inc.

Index of Poets and Poems

Index of First Lines

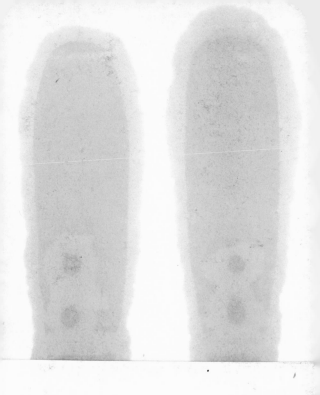

Northport Public Library
151 Laurel Avenue
Northport, New York
261-6930